DUDLEY PUBLIC LIBRARIES

The loan of this book may be renewed if not required by other readers, by contacting the library from which it was borrowed.

Aamer Hussein

ANOTHER GULMOHAR TREE

TELEGRAM

London San Francisco Beirut

ISBN: 978-1-84659-056-6

Copyright © Aamer Hussein, 2009

This first edition published in 2009 by Telegram

A full CIP record for this book is available from the British Library.
A full CIP record for this book is available from the Library of Congress.

Manufactured in Lebanon

TELEGRAM
26 Westbourne Grove, London W2 5RH
825 Page Street, Suite 203, Berkeley, California 94710
Tabet Building, Mneimneh Street, Hamra, Beirut
www.telegrambooks.com

For Mai

Unforgettable

Usman's Song

1

The sun had risen higher in the sky. Usman, who had guarded the farmer's field and chased away the crows all morning, was hot and hungry. He decided to eat his meal in the shade of a tree. Where, though, would he find a tree with leafy branches?

He walked a little and came to a gulmohar tree, flowerless but green enough to offer shelter. Beside the tree was a pond, which seemed to have filled up recently with rainwater, though it hadn't rained for days.

Usman took out his millet pancake, his pickles, and his flask of buttermilk.

Once again, his aunt had given him stale bread and rancid buttermilk. He was eating and drinking when he felt something tickle his left knee.

He looked down.

A little green frog was perched there.

Spare a little of your bread and milk for me.

The voice was so low he thought he'd imagined it.

Yes, it's me. He heard the voice again.

Frogs eat dragonflies.

But I'd like some bread and milk today.

Even if frogs don't talk, he said to himself, or eat bread and milk, what harm will it do to share my meal with a hungry creature?

My milk is sour milk and my pancakes are hard, but share my meal with me.

He broke off a piece of pancake dipped in buttermilk.

The frog ate and hopped away.

The food and the heat made Usman sleepy. He closed his eyes, and dreamed that the tree he was sitting under was laden with golden flowers that were raining down on him.

He shook himself awake. The tree was as it had been: there were no flowers in sight, but beside him was a pile of golden coins.

The next morning, Usman set off for the fields again. Had his meeting with the frog been a dream?

He couldn't resist returning to the tree when it was time for him to eat. The frog was waiting.

This time, it ate more than half his pancake dipped in more than half his bowl of buttermilk, before it hopped back into the pond.

Then Usman slept, and again the flowers fell on him, and again a pile of gold coins gleamed beside him when he awoke.

On the third day, he asked the frog: Are you under a spell? An evil spirit? A good one?

I'm just a frog, the little green creature said.

And have you been paying me in gold for the scrap of stale bread and the drop of sour milk I give you?

No, the frog said. Where would a green frog find gold?

And it hopped back into the pond.

On the fourth day, Usman went to his tree by the pond earlier than usual.

He had asked his aunt to make more bread that morning, and to give him a flask of fresh milk. But she had refused.

Where do you expect me to buy more flour from, with the pittance you give me?

The aunt was a thin childless woman whose husband had gone to war and never returned. She'd brought up Usman, her husband's orphaned nephew, on kicks, slaps and curses. She had never approved of Usman's work or the meagre income he brought home. He had planned to keep the coins he had found by his side hidden from her eyes, but couldn't resist doing what he did next. He laughed loudly and put a coin in her hand.

Use all the flour you have in the house today. And buy as much flour as you need.

There isn't any flour. You'll have to make do with stale bread.

On his way to the field, Usman stopped at the baker's

and at the cowherd's. He bought soft sweet bread and filled up his flask with milk fresh from the cow's udder.

When he reached the tree, the frog wasn't there.

Usman sang a song:

> Frog, Frog, feast on sweet bread
> Wash down with milk.
> Millet and barley, corn and wheat,
> Frog, Frog come eat your fill!

There was no response. He sang his song again.

Miss Frog, please!

And there she was, emerging from the pond.

On the sixth day, Usman woke with a heavy head.

You can't go to work today, his aunt said. You've been ill and raving all night. Here's some hot milk. I'll go to the fields in your place.

She draped herself in a mud-coloured shawl.

On the seventh day, when Usman went to his tree, the

pond was dry. The frog wasn't there. He sang his song. The frog didn't appear. He sang and he sang. The frog still didn't appear. And then it rained as it hadn't rained in three years.

2

A deer wandered into Rokeya's garden.

Where had it come from? There were no deer in the city, and no woods nearby.

Rokeya fed the deer on bread and milk. It followed her everywhere, like a puppy would. Sometimes even into the house.

Thirty-three days went by.

One day she came back from school, ran into the garden, and found the deer had gone.

Its real masters had come to take it home, her mother said. It belonged to a boy who had missed his pet so much he had fallen ill. The boy's father had gone to every gate in the neighbourhood, looking for his child's deer. They lived just two lanes away.

Rokeya cried for a week. She didn't eat. She wanted to die.

3

Umar, Bilal and Jani were hitting a wooden ball with poles. It rolled into the reeds by the bank of the river. They searched for it in the tall reeds. Mud squelched between their toes. Jani found a great mossy log and poked at it with her pole. It moved, suddenly, and snapped its jaws. They'd woken a sleeping crocodile.

They left the ball among the reeds and ran.

Umar, Bilal and Jani were the children of a well-to-do farmer. Once all the farmers of the seven villages around the river had paid tithes to the river's crocodiles and their king, to save their fields from being trampled down. They'd thrown the carcasses of freshly killed buffaloes, goats and young camels by the water for the reptiles to feed on. But then the crocodiles had become toothless and lost their bite. The farmers failed to pay their dues, or from time to time told the tanners to leave the skinned remains of old dead donkeys for the crocodiles' feasts.

The story of the crocodiles and their king had never been forgotten, though people had long since ceased to believe it. Now it was revived again, as the freshly planted corn and wheat were trampled on and torn from the soil by the crocodile army night after night while the farmers slept.

Two days later, the children's father had a visit from a man in a big green coat.

There's one way to avert this disaster, he said. Leave the girl, who insulted our commander by poking at him with a pole, on the bank of the river where you once left the carcasses of freshly killed buffaloes, goats and young camels. But you must tie the girl to a tree, and she must be alive.

The farmer wept all night, but he wouldn't, he swore, give his daughter to the river creatures.

When they woke at dawn, Jani fell at her father's feet.

> Take me to the river. Tie me to a tree.
> Give me to the crocodiles, if that's my destiny.

4

Usman sat beneath the tree and sang his song. The frog didn't emerge from the overflowing pond.

The days went by as he sat there, until the bread he had brought was as hard as the stones around him and the milk in his flask had turned sour.

He kept on singing.

You shouldn't make pets of wild things, Rokeya's mother said. When I was a child a peacock flew into our garden. It stayed for three days on our roof, dancing and screeching, until the father of the lonely children to whom it belonged came to take it away.

No, you must never make pets of wild things. No deer, no peacocks, they long for their forests and the longing brings bad luck.

But Rokeya had seen the peacock spread its fan. Its colours shone like mirrors in the sun.

6

The crocodiles kept their promise: they didn't return to the fields.

Jani's mother followed her to the river.

And when he thought that his wife and his daughter had both drowned, Jani's father too went to the river, to look for their remains.

7

And Usman kept on singing.

When Rokeya woke one morning she saw the tree in golden flower and the pond reflecting a clear, bright sky.

Today, she thought, I'll go back to school.

9

The farmer came back from the land of crocodiles.

In crocodile land, he told his sons, the crocodiles look like brave tall men, and their commander is the handsomest among them all. Your sister is the commander's bride. She sits in a green gauze dress on a swing of gold with her baby in a golden crib beside her. She sews gossamer shirts for her children, decorated with shells. Around her, crocodile girls in green velvet dresses with green mermaid hair sing watersongs and strum their mother-of-pearl lutes. Your mother eats sweets made of curds and syrup all day and her seven grandchildren play around her.

He took his older son with him when he left.

Umar stayed to watch the farm.

10

And Usman kept singing his song.

11

Bilal came back from the land of crocodiles.

In crocodile land, he told his brother, our parents are happy, and I was happy. When I return, you must come with me. Your sister misses you.

12

On her way back from school, Rokeya stopped by at the house of the boy whose father had come to take away her deer.

What did you do to my deer? he said. When it came back from your garden it refused to eat or drink. And one morning it lay down on the wet grass and died.

But now I have a puppy, a budgie and two rabbits.

13

And when the proud man whose seven vineyards had been devastated by the flood went to visit his poor neighbour who had lived on dried dates and water all winter to see how his trees had fared after the torrent he saw that the other's date palms were laden with fruit.

14

The bread is rock-hard, the milk is sour ...

15

The poor man gave his rich neighbour a sack of ripe dates.

Come back for more whenever you need them, he said.

16

Umar saw Bilal's skin turn greener every day.

Take me back to the river, the sick boy told his brother.

But you're too ill to travel.

So carry me to the river on your back, Bilal said. I need some bread from crocodile land. Or I'll die.

17

Rokeya, under the gulmohar, in the rain ...

18

And Usman keeps singing, singing.

The pond overflows.

Rokeya, sitting at its edge eating salted tamarind, dips her feet in the cool water, though she's not supposed to. She feels something tickle her knee.

What, no bread, no milk? Children should be eating bread and milk, not sour tamarind!

Rokeya looks down to see a little green frog perched on her left knee. It has a missing leg.

How did you find your way here?

I came in a bucket. What do you think? Frogs do swim, you know.

Why bread and milk? It's so boring. But you can share my tamarind.

Boring for you, maybe. But I'm hungry and I don't want tamarind. The seeds would choke me.

What will you give me if I bring you some bread and milk from the cook in the kitchen?

You're a bold little girl. I'll give you a gold coin or tell you my story.

Keep your coin and I'll take your story.

20

The crocodiles' bread was green, made of weed and lichen mixed with river water and the minced flesh of river creatures. It had a mossy smell.

Umar couldn't eat it, or drink from the pitchers of green river water in his sister's house. He lived on the bread and buttermilk he'd brought with him from home.

He watched Jani, surrounded by her crocodile girls and her crocodile brood, he saw her long jaw snapping.

His parents dragged their long green tails in the mud.

Bilal was turning greener. His skin was covered in scales.

My bread will soon finish and I've drunk all my milk. Come home with me now, Umar said. He circled his brother's wrist with his fingers. Come away before we grow tails.

21

On the sixth day, I heard the singing. I thought he was
ill. His throat must be sore, as his voice was low and
hoarse, not sweet and high as it had always been. But I
came to the edge of the pond. Today he was wrapped in
a mud-coloured shawl. He was almost still, just swaying
slightly. I hopped up to him, I sat on his knee. But the
bread he gave me was ash, and the milk was fiery. Then
he tore off his shawl and it wasn't my friend Usman at
all. In his place was a sourfaced woman. She said: You'd
try to buy my boy from me with coins of gold, would
you? I followed him here yesterday and saw your games,
witch. I gave him opium so that he'd sleep the sleep of
the dead. But the wretch woke up as I was leaving. Now
I'll give you bread and milk, you imp, and send you back
to the devil, your master. I crept away, away from her,
fainting. But as I escaped her claws, she broke off one
of my legs. When I stumbled into my pond, I fell on
stones. My pond was dry.

22

The proud man laments.

Where did I go wrong, Lord? What happened to my vineyards, which I bought with gold I'd earned from my own hard work? My vines, which a thousand poor men toiled long and hard to cultivate? And why did you afflict me with floods and spare my poor lazy neighbour and his date palm tree?

His neighbour says a prayer of thanks.

Then he dips dried dates in milk and hums a happy song.

23

I'll take you to your friend, Rokeya said to the frog.
Come, sit on my shoulder, and I'll take you there. I hear
him singing every morning.

She placed the frog in the curve of her shoulder, in
the shelter of her long hair.

She walks.

Listen!

Feast your fill , your fill ...

They heard the distant echo of Usman's song.

24

For thirty-three days, through cloud and wind and rain
and thunderstorm, Umar swam across rivers and walked
across fields with the weight of his brother Bilal on his
shoulder. The muscles of his arms and legs were seized
with cramps. The palms of his hands and the soles of
his feet were studded with thorns and gravel. At times
he thought he'd die of fatigue.

O Master of Mercy, he whispered. Lead us home.
And let the rain wash away the green scales from our
skin.

On the thirty-third day they saw, at a distance, the
palm tree and the gulmohar that marked the boundary
of home.

25

Under the gulmohar tree, golden petals falling all around him, Usman keeps singing his song.

Another Gulmohar Tree

1

When friends asked how long ago and where they'd first met, he would recall:

'A socialist seminar, in 1949, at some lecture theatre in Bloomsbury, I think. Bertrand Russell was speaking.'

'No, Bertrand Russell's talk was much later,' she'd correct him. 'We met at Senate House near Russell Square, and the year was 1950. Later, tea and biscuits were served. You were one of the main speakers at a symposium, and I was merely a face in the crowd.'

Their meeting had taken place on an evening in early March. The hall was so cold that many people in the audience, relieved to find shelter from the rain, had kept on their coats. Lydia was there with her friend Jack, who had served briefly in India just after the war. Usman was representing Pakistan, still a very young nation, to a group of other intellectuals from Ireland, Indonesia, India and Egypt who were discussing the situation in their countries. The lively debate on national liberation, as the student magazines later described it, was actually more of a tournament, and at times showed signs of turning into a fist-fight, with dissenting opinions about the moral rights and wrongs of the division of India and of Palestine.

Though Usman was the only Pakistani on the platform, and had been asked to speak about his country's aspirations, he belonged to no group or faction. He was in national dress, a long black coat with a high cropped collar, fitted waist and slits on the side, worn over a white shirt, its cuffs emerging from under his coat sleeves, and voluminous white trousers. He had a tall black woolly hat on his head. His shoes, she noticed, were laced and Western.

It was left to Usman to uphold the honour of his country against his Cambridge-educated Indian assailant Dr Pratap Dongre, a well-known representative of his country's ruling Congress Party, who thought that the creation of Pakistan was a conspiracy, hatched by a posse of fanatics.

Lydia, in the audience, was moved by the passion with which the Pakistani speaker, articulating his country's position, argued that new eras created new nations and ordinary people in such circumstances performed as both kings and as pawns on the chessboard of history. She was even more impressed with the quiet dignity of his public manner. An ardent reader of Yeats, she understood, for the first time, the poet's lines about the best and the worst, their intensity or lack of conviction. Some impulse made her decide to tell him how much she had learned from what he said.

Though she was the granddaughter of a Georgian émigré, Lydia had never before had a significant conversation with such a dark foreigner. But something about his haunted cheekbones, and his bewildered eyes shadowed by stray locks of greying hair, intrigued her.

In turn, he, who had largely avoided contact with foreign women before, was drawn to the friendly manner and clear, low-pitched voice of this forthcoming but shy young woman with dark hair, candid grey-green eyes and broad square shoulders. Though she was dressed sensibly in a mannish navy blue jacket with gold buttons, he noticed that she wore pearl studs in her pierced ears, and a pearl-encrusted gold brooch was pinned to her lapel.

'I'm an illustrator – book jackets, magazine articles, children's stories, that sort of thing,' she informed him. (She would never have dared to describe herself as an artist.)

As she might have guessed, he was a journalist by trade.

'I'm here in London on a year's secondment to the foreign desk of the *Daily Telegraph*,' he told her. His English, she'd noticed when he gave his speech, was syntactically adequate and quite rich in vocabulary, but his conversation was hesitant, halting. 'I'll be leaving at the end of May. And your name is …?'

'Lydia Javashvili.'

'Miss … Joshili?' He stumbled.

'You can call me Lydia,' she said, holding out her hand with a smile that moved him.

'Usman Ali Khan.'

He took her extended hand, but he didn't ask her to call

him by his first name, which was relatively easy to say. Later, she'd hear his colleagues refer to him as Usman Sahib in the common Pakistani way, which, he explained to her, meant Mr Usman, and she took to calling him Mr Usman until the end of their days together.

And she'd learn that the mess he'd made of her surname was deliberate: Joshili meant plucky in his language.

༄

Getting to know each other was easy after that first encounter.

When they met at the British Museum to see the mummies three weeks later, she suggested they visit the Victoria and Albert the following Saturday. The weather was milder, almost balmy; she had taken trouble to prepare a picnic hamper to carry to Kensington Palace Gardens.

'Tell me more about your life,' she said, by the grassy banks of a lemon-coloured Serpentine.

'And what would you like to know?' He looked puzzled.

'Everything,' she said with a comic gesture.

She had enough questions, some of them naive. She continued to pose them, and listened to his answers, at Kew Gardens, Windsor Castle and other places she took him to see on the Saturday and Sunday afternoons he had off. Spring drew closer, and cherry blossom appeared on bare branches.

2

He was born, he told her, in a village in the Punjab, and brought up by his maternal grandparents in Multan, as his mother had died when he was a child and his father refused to know him. He was educated in the vernaculars at home; his grandfather, a herbalist, had some knowledge of Persian and Arabic, which he imparted to the willing boy.

At twelve, when his grandfather died, he was sent away to Rawalpindi, to live with his father, who was finally obliged to accept him. He didn't like his stepmother (she had, it emerged, been his father's clandestine second wife before the death of Usman's mother). Nor did he share much sympathy with his younger siblings: in this house that should have been his own he felt like an unwanted guest at a meal or an unwelcome stranger.

His father, she learned, had sent him to work at his uncle's bicycle shop when he was fourteen. His days of studying were over. But he had brought several of his grandfather's books with him, which he read whenever he could, randomly acquainting himself with the great works of Urdu and Persian, immersing himself in the verses of Momin, Meer, Ghalib, the classic epic and romantic poems of Ferdausi, Jami,

Nizami and Ameer Khusrau. He supplemented his income by helping the children of richer people with their studies. More often, he'd found himself instructing those with less than himself, adults among them, to read and write.

Usman was eighteen when his father found him a bride, within their extended family. Naimat Bibi was older, the only living child of a well-to-do father; her brother had died in his teens, of a lingering ailment of the lung. Usman's father saw the marriage he had arranged for his son as the perfect solution: he'd be rid of a dependant and an unworthy, inefficient employee who spent most of his time reading and couldn't repair a wheel. He would also supply an older cousin with a son. Usman's real job as Sharif Din's son-in-law was to provide him with an heir; in return for comfortable lodgings, good food and a respectable social position, he was expected to serve as the older man's secretary and companion. Usman's wife and he were never compatible – they could barely spend time together without Usman becoming aware of her disdain, and Naimat Bibi of his indifference. But because he was young and entirely without experience of women, they became the parents of twin sons within fifteen months.

At twenty-one, Usman said farewell to his family and set off to seek his own fortune. He had started to write poems in a very traditional mode and had submitted them to journals in Lahore; they were accepted almost immediately for publication. Tempted by his success, he left for the big city, where the ingenuity and persistence of youth enabled him to find work in the office of an Urdu newspaper, and to continue, in his spare time, to write.

But leaving Rawalpindi also meant giving up the traditional verses he had so blithely written. From the start, he recognised his subject, which was life as he knew it: not only the story of his own fairly difficult circumstances, on which he based the sentimental novel that was his first book, but those of the people he'd known, many of them unkind and mercenary, others simple, good folk who life had treated less fairly than their virtuous deeds and their faith in divine justice deserved.

For four years he had been posted to Delhi, where his gruff accent and provincial manners caused him to become the butt of literary jokes. But he was also cast by the literati as the naive storyteller from the Punjab who had access to the folklore and indigenous wisdom (or folly) that were just becoming fashionable in fiction. And during those four years in the imperial capital he acquired many of its refinements of nuance and gesture, just as he'd learnt, in Lahore, to wear Western clothes with an air of unstudied elegance.

In Delhi, too, the ways of the foreign rulers deepened his dislike of them, instilled in him when he'd first listened to shadowy accounts of the Jalianwala massacre. Certain activities of his had caused the authorities to throw him into jail for several months; he was never very keen to divulge these to Lydia, but she guessed, after reading some books on recent Indian history she found in the library, that he'd been a conscientious objector to the conscription of Indian youths from poor villages as soldiers for World War II. During his imprisonment he contracted tuberculosis, which had weakened his lungs for the rest of his life.

When he emerged from the prison sanatorium, he was jobless. He decided to try his luck again in Lahore. Even after a separation of several years, his friends there thought well of him, and imprisonment as an anti-colonial radical had given him a certain glamour. The extreme polish his Urdu had acquired in Delhi, evident in the uninflected sentences he wrote, was highly effective in his journalism. So was his working knowledge of English; several of his tasks required a translator's skill. In the short stories he was writing, which he had realised were the real expression of his gift, his tone could, however, seem bald, and his quiet timbre shocking.

Some of this Lydia, who didn't know a word of Urdu, pieced together from his infuriatingly modest accounts, although he did explain to her that his own desire to rid himself of the provincial inflection that echoed in the writings of his Punjabi contemporaries made him write in the manner his critics variously described as flat, laconic or lapidary.

Sometimes he'd recount to her the gist of stories he had written, or those he still wanted to write. He had written a little about London: pinched, shabby and hag-ridden with post-war austerities though it was, it still remained a city where people would save on necessities to buy themselves a book, a ticket to the Proms or a bunch of hyacinths.

Distance had only sharpened his vision of the land he'd

left behind. In writing of his native place the looser, rougher language of his youth would come back to him, more musical and full of metaphors; he was experimenting with stories composed almost entirely of dialogue, to allow his characters to speak in their own voices.

He'd written, too, about the independence of his country, which mattered a lot to him, but, he said, he could only write about it with a light touch. Partition, he explained, he'd witnessed vicariously, not having been at a site of catastrophe: he'd moved to Karachi in the mid-1940s to distance himself from his family for ever. He continued, however, to send money to his wife and sons. In 1947 he'd seen some rich Sindhi Hindus leave for Bombay, and some wealthy Muslims from Bombay, the United Provinces and Hyderabad take their homes and their position. But what had touched him most were the accounts of the ignorant and the simple who travelled enormous distances, sometimes on foot, to make their homes in a new land; some chased away from their native places, but many, too, who'd come in pursuit of their dreams. He'd written a little book about them, their fortitude and perseverance, without the darkness of his left-wing contemporaries' accounts.

As to his own allegiances, there was no doubt: he'd never even thought that he wouldn't make his life in the new Pakistan.

ॐ

'The first time I saw snow here: I drew my curtain at 7 in

the morning and it was coming down in flakes as big as the palm of your hand. The trees were capped in snow, and the tops of buses, and a man in a coat went by looking like a walking snowman. And another, with an umbrella, looked like a snowy scarecrow. I went to work in that weather, slipping and sliding …'

'… but now that you're in London, haven't you even considered staying on, at least a little longer than just the year allotted to you?'

'And what would I do here?'

This was only one of the many questions she put to him that evoked a puzzled or bemused response.

She tentatively suggested they should collaborate on a translation of some of his stories she thought she might send to an acquaintance who worked for a left-wing journal. (After all, Mulk Raj Anand and Ahmed Ali had been lauded by Bloomsbury, encouraged by Forster, and published here before the war. Usman could dictate English versions, she suggested, which she'd type and improve.)

'I just couldn't convey the voices in my head in English,' he answered. 'And who'd want to know about my people here?'

His written English, a third language which he had only acquired in Delhi in his twenties, was clear and sharp but occasionally stilted. One day Lydia asked, over a cup of tea at Lyons, why he had never attempted to write fiction in it. He responded: 'I can't even write in Punjabi, my mother tongue! You don't choose the language you write in, it chooses you.'

The language of Lydia's craft was, of course, the language of colours and forms. Green woods and water meadows, ducks and swans, horses and sheep: the familiar sights of Hampshire, where she had spent much of her childhood, had opened her eyes to the world around her and made her want to paint. Often, though, she'd felt that her eyes, captivated by what they saw, kept her living in a continuous present tense which was devoid of longing for anything other than its own pleasures; then again, the wistful whites, greens and blue-greys she used to paint her lakes, ponds and rivers, and the lonely smallness of the people inhabiting her scenes, carried within them a sense of something beyond the immediacy of what her vision framed.

Often, alone, she wondered whether written words came from a different place – of memory, perhaps – that didn't depend on the eyes at all. She searched for the words to speak of these things to him, but she'd stutter and fall silent, or ask him about his stories instead, though she sometimes felt that he would tell her his stories merely because she asked, and because they were just about the only thing in creation that carried him away.

She, too, was writing a little, but she felt he didn't take her aspirations very seriously. Once she said, 'I've been working on a story about an English woman who falls in love with an Egyptian,' disguising the fact that she was writing about the two of them, and he asked: 'Working? For your friend's paper, you mean? It must be quite hard for the couple, who are they, friends of yours?'

৯

So she talked about herself, and her stories beguiled him, especially when they walked in the park or by the river as evening shadows deepened.

She started in reverse, telling him about her war years, how she'd made maps for the Ministry of Information, then joined the Women's Auxiliary Air Force and received a commendation for bravery. She told him about her comfortable childhood, spent between Chiswick and Hampshire, though she felt there was little to tell. Her half-Georgian father, a respectable banker, had spent a lifetime trying to be English but retained, somewhere, a longing for lost rivers and routes. Her Scottish mother was devoutly Catholic. She had four brothers and sisters. Her comfortable though slightly stifling upbringing had always left her feeling out of step with the world; she had broken away when the war began, to seek a new life for herself at the age of nineteen.

There was much that she elided, perhaps more than he did. During the war she'd married: Mark Beecham was a fighter pilot with medals and an attendant arrogance which contrasted with his well-heeled blandness. They'd lasted two years on the wings of desires born of her virginal inexperience and his war-fuelled desperation. When she fell pregnant and decided to abort her child, she was crash-landed in a quagmire of misunderstanding and recrimination, particularly as she knew he'd been seeing a number of other women. As a cradle Catholic, she'd committed one mortal sin. And to add divorce to that? Unthinkable. An annulment, then? On what grounds?

But would the church even recognise her marriage? Her mother never had. Her father was an agnostic born into the Orthodox sect; she had married Mark in a registry office, promising, because of her mother's pleas, to convert her Protestant husband to Catholicism, and have a church wedding with all the requisite rituals when things were more peaceful.

She decided on divorce. Her residual guilt, too, went along with her married name, the way so many things were going in the aftermath of the war.

She told Usman she'd be thirty on the 9th of April. He remarked: 'And a pretty young woman like you, not married?' 'My divorce will soon be coming through,' she responded. She was unwilling, though, to admit that her father had helped her to rid herself of Mark by paying him to stage an adulterous encounter (with a streetwalker rather than one of his paramours) and by promising that Lydia wouldn't ask for alimony.

3

When Usman was with Lydia, everything seemed spontaneous and natural, even the long silent lapses in their conversations. She lived by the Regent's Canal, in a tall narrow house owned by her two great-aunts, who had made a genteel compromise with diminishing finances by renting rooms to students or young working women; they refused to take rent from her, but she helped with expenses. Often, in the evening, he'd stroll almost all the way back with her and leave her at the corner of Blomfield Road, feeling at ease with himself and with his thoughts of her. But at work, or waiting at the bus stop to Oxford Circus or walking home from Marylebone Station, alone in the vanilla evenings that refused to shade into night, with his mind fixed on his return to Karachi, he'd ask himself questions to which he had no answer. What awaited him in the seaside city he had chosen as his home, he, a man who had no home because he'd lost his birthplace long ago and never learnt to belong anywhere else, what would he do with his life in that open city teeming with strangers like himself? Yet those strangers would speak to him in his language and, perhaps, think his thoughts. What, on the other hand, could he expect from this other city, this imperial dowager without a throne who had allowed him into her precincts, and neither demanded anything of him nor gifted him very much apart from an unexpected friendship? And what did this woman he thought of as his friend, until so very recently a stranger, see in him? What was he to her, a curiosity, a repository of stories, an exotic trophy, something to allay her sense of Western guilt? No, he would reflect, she was a friend and someone who, a stranger in this city of strangers and oddly lonely like himself, had reached out to him, not out of any sense of pity or even curiosity, but in search of a companion to talk to, all through the long damp late spring days.

'Is this where our paths separate, then, Mr Usman?' In three days he would be leaving. 'Or is there somewhere left for us to go?'

'I'm eleven years older than you.' He'd been quiet for a quarter of an hour, so long that she thought he'd taken her words literally, and she hadn't tried to fill the silence with a question or a quip. 'And even though I've been separated from my wife for longer than I ever lived with her, she and my sons are still my responsibility. I can't offer you anything. I don't feel I even have the right to speak to you of affection. But I'll never forget what you've given me. I was alone, a stranger in a strange country, I felt like a ghost in the rain and the cloud and the snow ... as if I didn't have a presence or even a body, and you ... you drew me out of myself, you brought a little ... brightness into my life. You have my regard, my friendship and my gratitude, for ever.'

She found herself wondering, as she had often done before, whether he translated his hesitant, measured phrases from his own language; they sounded as if he'd written them out before he said them. She smiled and put her hand on his, to conceal the expression on her face that exposed, she was sure, a feeling of rejection.

He must like her more than a little; he had spent so much time with her. But he hadn't once pretended he wanted to stay on in England. He found the city dank and its architecture morose, and most of all he hated the leafless winter. He even complained that the wet green of London parks was monotonous, and summer days that ended hours after the 6 o'clock sunsets he was used to were far too long after the ominous darkness of the cold months.

She didn't doubt that he saw his future in his own country, among his people, speaking his language. And she, who had never thought in negative ways about foreigners – after all, her grandfather was one – could she ever present Usman to her family as her life's companion, this man from such a distant place, so different from anything they knew or recognised?

There was also the question of their different faiths. Although she still believed in a guiding principle that was, when she thought about it, benign, she certainly wouldn't have considered religion a matter of any personal concern. But his religion evidently meant something to Usman:

though he didn't pray regularly, he often spoke of its humane aspects and its egalitarian values. He wouldn't touch alcohol, preferred not even to enter a pub, and, as for food, not only did he avoid every part of the pig, but would keep insisting that bread, biscuits, ice cream and various other foods were tainted with its fat. As a consequence he lived on fruit and cereals, except when they could eat Indian food.

She liked the cooking and the atmosphere at Veeraswamy's, the fancy Indian restaurant on Swallow Street, where you could see patrician-seeming ladies in diaphanous saris, with their well-groomed husbands, entertaining English dignitaries. That restaurant was, most of the time, too expensive for the working people Usman and Lydia were. But Usman was a regular at two canteens that served Indian food to students and starving expats. When they entered those places, dimly lit, smoky basements with tin ashtrays placed on white-topped tables often sticky with the remains of the last diner's meal, Lydia would be surprised by how intimate her shy-seeming companion was with his colleagues and compatriots of all ages, and how well they received him.

At first, when they saw her in his company, they made comments she couldn't understand. Awkward silences followed the rounds of hugs and handshakes, and the tacit understanding was that Usman and his lady friend would sit at a table apart.

And then, gradually, in the weeks before Usman left for Karachi, one friend after another would approach their table, join them for a cup of tea, and offer or ask for cigarettes (both she and Usman were smokers). It became evident that she'd been accepted as a sympathetic presence and, at least tentatively, as Usman's companion.

Her own acquaintances were more casual. One said Usman looked like a gipsy, another remarked how well he used his fork and knife considering, and yet another that he sounded like a Scotsman or a Russian. Suddenly, these people she had liked, for some of whom she'd felt affection, were unfamiliar and lacking in understanding or sympathy; she knew that they all dismissed her friendship with him as her gesture of rebellion, her transient fancy, while some, even more oddly, cast him as a benign Othello to her Desdemona.

But no, not everyone. Her friend Jack, the left-wing journalist, met Usman for the first time at the premiere of a new Terence Rattigan play for which he had given them free tickets. 'Are you his mistress?' he asked her, a few days later. They were lunching at a pub near Green Street. She snorted and nearly choked.

'I thought not.' Jack lit a cigarette. 'You're perfectly matched, the pair of you. Puzzled angels, visiting earth on holiday, lost until you finally find each other.'

The evening before he left, Usman cried a little as they walked away from the restaurant he'd chosen for their farewell dinner – the fancy Indian one on Swallow Street – and she asked him to take her to his lodgings. He lived in a lane off the Marylebone Road. The spring night was fresh if slightly cool; they walked all the way. They stayed up till first light and embraced and kissed each other's cheeks and lips for what seemed like hours. But he slept on the sofa. In the morning, she saw him off, dry-eyed, at Waterloo Station. To go to the port, to watch him board his ship, would have meant too much. They'd exchanged addresses at dawn over squares of buttered toast and cups of the tea he'd stewed with milk and sugar until it tasted like syrup. They'd said they'd keep in regular touch. That was the only promise.

4

In later years, she enjoyed telling her children the tale of how she took a ship to Karachi two years after he left England.

I was on the tube, she said, travelling to work on a February day, hanging on to a railing, inhaling the staleness of unaired winter coats, unwashed hair and egg-and-bacon breakfast breath, and I decided to cross the seas to visit your father. I had no future plans, no expectations. I just knew I had to see him.

(There was some truth in her story – she didn't dare to expect anything, and she had been imagining the voyage out as she travelled to work – but if she had wanted to, she could have been more meticulous about retracing the itinerary of her decision. Finding her interest in her work abating until she took only the odd commission to draw a picture to accompany a love story in a woman's weekly, or a sketch of a Christmas pudding or a knitting pattern. Reading the Marmaduke Pickthall translation of the Qur'an she'd bought, the life of Muhammad and, with even more interest, accounts of Muslim women's lives: Nabia Abbott's *Aishah, the Beloved of Mohammed*, Margaret Smith's tales of the mystic Rabia of Basra. Studying Urdu [or Hindoostawney, as her teacher called it] with retired, red-faced Major MacGregor who, when he left Hinjer as he lovingly remembered it, had lost most connections with the land in which he'd spent his youth, and longed to share the language he'd learnt so intimately. Saving carefully, and selling her grandmother's gold-and-ruby brooch to make up the difference in passage.)

She was losing patience. Usman's gracious but remote letters offered no promise of reunion, showed no sense of loss; but then he would evoke, among pithy accounts of the lonely, work-obsessed life he led in Karachi, some tender memory. I wish I could see you again, he'd written in his most recent letter. That was enough (he was, after all, a writer) to reassure her that their time together hadn't been a lonely man's diversion or a whim, and certainly not motivated by lust, as he'd never touched her until that very last night, and even then he'd only embraced her after she'd reached out to him first. But was it love he felt for her? Wasn't the physical distance he'd maintained between them till that last night a sign that he had seen her only as a friend, a good listener, an adequate conversationalist – certainly not his life's companion?

She would have become his lover, had he wanted her to; having given her virginity to a man she didn't love, and that within the zone of marriage, she would have willingly made love with someone she cared for even if, in the end, it meant no more than a few nights' passion. In the first few months after Usman left, she'd met some men while she waited for a sign from him – dined out, danced, accepted gifts, even toyed with the possibility of a kiss or two until, at the last minute, she'd quickly turned her face so that importunate lips would dampen her ear or her cheek.

Then he'd written to say his wife had 'passed away, God rest her soul'. Her own divorce had come through so quietly that she'd felt tempted to phone Mark, now that he was her ex-husband, and ask if she could take him out to celebrate. Instead she'd phoned her father, who met her for lunch at his London club on Sackville Street. He didn't say very much, but he gave her £50 in ten crisp notes in a white envelope. Then she met Jack. Go, Jack told her, and forced her to take £10 from him. Go before your life turns grey on you.

On the boat, during the fortnight that it took to sail to Karachi, she'd often wonder: how welcome would a pale foreigner be in a country which had only recently rid itself of the unwanted presence of her kind? And would she herself now seem, in his own country, too much of a stranger to Usman?

She arrived in Karachi on a Monday, to be met at the harbour by an acquaintance's sister-in-law, a very kind woman called Claire, whose husband Richard happened to be working there for a large pharmaceutical concern. It was evening, the sky was reddish, and a smell of crayfish hung in the air, to be replaced by a smokier smell, like burning wood, as they drove past some very tall colonial buildings and what seemed to be Orientalised Gothic constructions into what Claire told her was the business centre of town.

Claire's green-gabled two-storey house was on a tree-lined avenue called Victoria Road that could have been in Europe, except that every third or fourth tree was a palm tree. Lydia had planned to stay at a hotel, wanting the freedom that choice would give her, though she knew her funds wouldn't keep her there for long. She'd arranged to move to the Metropole – in the centre of town but still quite close to where Claire lived – after two nights with her friend. She hoped her stay at the hotel wouldn't last longer than three or four nights.

On Wednesday morning, on the way from Elphinstone Street, where the smart shops were, to the more picturesque and colourful Bohri Bazaar, she stopped off at the office where she knew Usman worked, and sent her friend's chauffeur to drop off the note she'd written to him at dawn.

He was still at his desk at his lunch break, as usual drinking only a cup of over-boiled tea, with a couple of rusks to dip into the hot liquid, and a blood orange to follow. When the clerk brought him an unstamped, unsealed envelope, addressed in a familiar handwriting, he tried his best to remain calm, telling himself that Lydia must have sent the note with some friend visiting Karachi.

I'm at the Metropole (he read) *in Room 340. If I*

don't hear from you within two days, I'll leave for
Bombay. I've been offered a job there.

Her scrawl, then the sprawl of her signature.

When he'd read it, he felt the long night he'd lived in since he left her, of numb hopelessness, of anxious loneliness, slip away from him and turn, if not into day, then at least into tentative first light.

ॐ

He reached the Metropole as soon as he could get a rickshaw, which overcharged to take him there. It was a relatively quiet hour of the afternoon. He summoned her down to the lobby where he stood waiting, holding a welcoming garland of jasmine and roses for which he'd overpaid the urchin who sold flowers on the pavement outside his office. She was dressed in a white linen shirt that looked like a man's, with a very full turquoise skirt and a red belt. She looked taller and paler in this city, her bobbed brown hair fairer; she had lost some weight. I asked your mother to marry me on the spot! he told his children when they were growing up. (The truth was that he had proposed to her two days later, after taking her to the Clifton seafront, Gandhi Gardens, Frere Hall, and then to the sandy beaches miles away from town, all the sights that one foreigner in Karachi would take another foreigner to see, remembering all the while how she had introduced him to the hidden corners of London; he was still unsure if she was only in the city en route to

Bombay, or whether she had any intention, or reason, to remain here, which he now knew he wanted her to do. What he said was, Would you consider staying on here? And do what? she asked, quite rudely. Get a job as a nanny? No, he said. With me, as my wife.)

Although a slightly embarrassed Claire, along with her husband Richard, had agreed to chaperone her to her wedding, she would have had no one to act as her witness to their wedding two days later if Usman had not arranged for Chowdhry Nazir Ahmad, an elderly publisher who'd become his close friend and benefactor, to stand in the role of her father. At the brief, unsentimental wedding ceremony, the Qazi asked a certain Rokeya if she'd accept Usman as her husband. And Lydia, in perfectly comprehensible Urdu, said, I, Rokeya, accept. He couldn't conceal his surprise: the new name, the ease with the words. He hadn't asked her to convert. She'd quite simply taken the step herself, in London, and chosen a name she knew he loved.

It was only later he would tell her that she'd struck a slightly false note: no Muslim bride would have proclaimed her acceptance in quite so bold a manner.

5

She was enthralled from the start.

On one side of the city was sand-bordered sea. The other edge was desert: dust, rock, hill, an occasional ditch lying in wait for rain to make it a pond.

In the dusty, rocky part of town, far from the sea and Claire's colonial mansion and the Metropole hotel, they found the plot of land on which they built their little hilltop home. Here in this landscape miniature pink and yellow flowers bloomed wild on bushes, concealing black berries of a jammy sour-sweetness. Cactus and thorn bush thrived, but bougainvillaea found its natural habitat in this aridity, and jasmine, too, seemed to flower in wilderness, filling the evening air with its fragrance, somewhere between honey and clove.

And the gold-orange blossoms of the flame tree nestled like torches among bright, light-green leaves. Locals called the tree gulmohar, which, she worked out, meant 'flower-coin'. For a few weeks in early summer, it would flower so furiously that its branches, divested now of leaves, would seem from a distance as if they were on scarlet fire. She was surprised to find that, like herself and so many other inhabitants of her adopted city, the gulmohar, which appeared to be rooted in this soil, was a transplant; she read in a book about plants and flowers that the Royal Poinciana (its more prosaic botanical name) had originated in Madagascar.

There were creatures running around that she would never have recognised. Slender lizards in the grass seemed harmless enough to the country girl she had been, but crested chameleons that changed colour (once she brought one into the house on a flowering branch) and the monster-reptile they called 'go' that she saw once on a rock and supposed was a cousin of the iguana, gave her gooseflesh.

The ponds were full of grumbling frogs, the gardens of chirring cicadas. And birds she didn't know would suddenly appear along with the kites and the crows and the sparrows, darting down to drink from some flower. 'Hummingbird, brain fever bird, mynah bird, kingfisher, honeysuckle,' Usman would intone, and she'd slap his arm and tell him not to tease her because she knew that the honeysuckle was a flower, not a bird.

Unfamiliar odours could overwhelm you on summer days, from open sewers of rainbow liquids flowing like sluggish canals, from rotten fish used as manure for beds of sunflowers and roses in the gardens of the rich, from fruit ripening in the May sunshine.

People sold fruit of many shapes and sizes on the dusty sides of the wide artery road that led to the centre of the city, melons and grapes of colours she'd never seen, hard green pears and huge chartreuse apples, rosy mangoes, mottled yellow bananas and bright oranges in unimaginable numbers, pine nuts in their swarthy shells spilling over the edges of wicker baskets.

A grassy roundabout on the road to the centre of town was a riot of yellow and orange gerbera. Elsewhere, you could see half-naked children cavorting in ponds the colour of milky tea with lazy buffaloes lolling around them – until the diligent authorities paved over the ponds and made space for an elegant new residential area.

Rations and privation coexisted with material luxury and profusion. A fountain with water cascading over varicoloured lights in a public square played the theme music of a popular American film at certain times of the day. Cinemas showed the latest Hollywood and Pinewood productions. On elegant Elphinstone Street, the air-conditioned sari palace Sanaullah sold fabrics of unbelievable delicacy; next door, in stalls so narrow you could hardly fit a single person into them, friendly Chinese men measured your feet to make you shoes of the softest, finest leather. Upstairs, in large rooms with huge wooden tables, you could eat bowls of steaming noodles served by their brothers, taking pleasure in the slightly illicit pleasure of devouring crab claws and shark fins. Also on Elphinstone Street were the city's two biggest bookshops facing each other across the road, where on her rare trips to the centre of town she would pick up the books she'd never had time to read during the years of her desultory education: Gibbon, Plato, Graves's *Greek Myths*, Burton's *One Thousand and One Nights*. Occasionally, the latest lurid-jacketed Agatha Christie or Georgette Heyer paperback evoked a twinge of nostalgia, but was soon handed on to a friend because the fantasies of its author seemed so irrelevant to the concerns of her own life.

Sugar, rice and flour were strictly rationed, and meat available only five days a week, but milk fresh from the cow's udder was delivered in cans to your doorstep and fish and crustaceans of the most extravagant sorts were sold on stalls in the open market. Pereira's bakery in the shadow of the Roman Catholic cathedral served exquisite Mediterranean-inspired breads, pastries and cakes which, Usman told her, were made by the descendants of bakers trained long ago by the Portuguese.

In a world that she'd heard was strictly divided between the very rich and the very poor, most of the people she met – professionals, government servants, teachers, journalists – were, in her book of etiquette, neither very rich nor very poor but lower-middle or middle-middle class. The former lived in apartments or even tenements near and beyond the centre of town, or little houses in colonies far, far away in the suburbs; the latter – to which she and Usman, though somewhat tenuously, were seen to belong – built or rented their homes in sprawling residential 'societies'. These were usually single-storied houses with gardens of varying sizes, many of them built on government loans. These neighbourhoods – some modest, some more confidently displaying the financial assets of their residents – were, unlike the centre of the city and its older parts, signals and creations of a brave new capital, heedless of the past, free of traditional or colonial influence, built for their changed needs by its citizens according to their own blueprint. In the early days, longing for someone to listen to stories of her new home, she'd write long, detailed letters to Jack, but the letters would lie around, incomplete or unposted, and soon she found no time to write.

While Usman was working for the Government Publications Division, they had taken a loan to build their minuscule home – a four-room bungalow behind which was a crescent-shaped strip of grassy lawn with flower beds and a gulmohar tree, and a sliver of backyard. It had been constructed in a mere eight months, while acquaintances complained of having to wait up to three years for their residences to be ready. After they'd spent the first fifteen months of their married life in a little service bungalow in Napier Barracks near the centre of town which had running water for only an hour or two a day and a squat lavatory, the space both within and around their new house seemed luxurious. All around them, new houses were filling in empty spaces, in sober greys embellished with darker greys, combinations of rich Mediterranean ochre with beige or cream, pale pink, white with green or coral.

She had had their walls painted a pink-tinged white and her house was full of windows. She had decided to dispense with conventional Western furniture; influenced by the manner in which she'd seen Usman's arty friends decorate their rooms, she had divans made from scraps of wood and covered those and some low wooden chests with white cotton, bright swatches of cloth and pieces of rugs, or straw matting bought from the local markets, to serve as seats. Screens woven of straw served as curtains and to divide rooms in two after her three children were born. Usman and she slept on the floor on thin mattresses, covering themselves with patchwork quilts only during the six weeks of so-called winter.

In contrast to those she'd met in London, Usman's friends accepted her easily, addressing her as sister-in-law with affectionate regard as soon as they recognised her spontaneous interest in their lives, her keen willingness to play a part in the life of their city, her hospitality. Shopkeepers and shoppers in the Nursery, a twenty-minute walk away from their lane, soon became used to the friendly foreign woman with sunburnt arms and legs who, dressed in flimsy cotton shifts, shopped alone and filled her baskets with the oddest assortment of goods which she loaded on her bicycle.

But soon Rokeya, as Lydia now preferred to be known, changed her foreign clothes for local apparel. She found it easier to ride her bike to the shops dressed in loose trousers and a cotton tunic, her dopatta wrapped around her forehead and knotted at the nape of her neck to keep her hair from flying in her eyes, one end grazing a shoulder, the other streaming in the air behind her as she rode around the lanes.

6

Usman had changed jobs. Uncomfortable in a government post where he had begun to feel that some of his colleagues were being restricted in their freedom of expression and others were introducing cultural agendas he found reactionary, he resigned to take up a post Chowdhry Sahib, his publisher, friend and supporter, offered him as Editor-in-Chief of a new Urdu journal of culture, *Kal, Aaj aur Kal*. (Which meant, his wife wrote in amusement to her friend Jack, *Yesterday, Today and Tomorrow*.) The magazine's office was near Bunder Road. To make his journey easier, Chowdhry had given him a Volkswagen on almost permanent loan, which he soon learnt to drive himself. (Rokeya took driving lessons too. Her tendency to misread signals made her a hazard, though; even in their quiet neighbourhood she was twice stopped by the police. She soon stopped driving.)

Although socially conscious, interested in politics and radical in several of his sympathies, Usman had decided, as he reached middle age, to abstain from any overtly political activity. Neither would he collude with or uphold what he thought of as the power lobby, once he saw a new strain of corruption becoming at first insidious and then endemic.

His severe style and the unpretentious integrity of his vision had earned him the respect of other writers. The great poet Faiz had praised him more than once in print; the young but intimidating critic Mumtaz Shirin, herself an acclaimed short story writer, had compared the sound of his prose to brooklets of clear water running over rocks and stones in sunny weather.

Dressed in immaculately pressed trousers, wearing a tie even in summer though he would roll up the sleeves of the pale blue cotton shirts he favoured to the elbow and sling his jacket over his shoulder, Usman was a regular lecturer at literary forums and a sought-after guest at gatherings. His essays on every genre of literature, particularly those about classical Urdu poetry and traditional romances in Urdu and Punjabi, were gaining him a formidable reputation as a critic. But he hadn't reached the common reader with his recent fiction. Even his admirers made too much of the obscurity in which he wrote, somehow perpetuating the image of him as a recluse in a cave, or a rural storyteller who was out of touch with current trends.

And now Shah Bilal, another writer from a Punjabi background, had taken to reworking Usman's material in a far more sensational vein, melodramatic and condemnatory. Seven or eight years younger than Usman, he was given the kind of acclaim to which the older writer had never aspired. In 1936 he had sent a sheaf of stories to Usman, who was working in Lahore and had just published his first book; Bilal was nineteen then, and had robust, if somewhat rude, talent. Usman had endorsed a story for publication. For some years, Bilal had claimed Usman as his mentor; he spoke of a close tie between them that hadn't existed, as they had never once met in person. But when Bilal won a prestigious prize and accepted a post as cultural advisor to the government, his self-acknowledged debt to Usman was forgotten.

Bilal's prose was dense with mixed metaphors and had a folksy lyricism which displayed his origins as a songwriter for films. In public he declaimed his work with rhetorical flourishes, interspersing stories of his own rural background. (Though he claimed to be a poor farmer's son, he was actually the grandson of a landowner, and had attended university in Lahore.)

Usman felt, somehow, short-changed or cheated when he read yet another essay praising Bilal for his vulgar plagiarisms of just the sort of writings Usman had been publishing for nearly two decades, or when he saw himself compared, to his disadvantage, with the more flamboyant younger writer. The worst moment came on a brief visit to Lahore when he was invited to read at a function that, he had been told, was to be held in his honour by a literary acquaintance; he was kept waiting an hour and a half for Bilal, the Chief Guest, to arrive, and found that he had again been relegated to second best. Bilal, at this first-ever meeting of theirs, was gracious and full of compliments, and announced in his speech that, in the far-off days of his youth, he'd taken courage and direction from his respected older friend Usman's writings. But he made no mention of Usman's advice and help, or of the fact that in those early days of their career – indeed, until today – they had never met. Usman found it indiscreet to mention that he was only twenty-six and hardly an eminent man of letters when he'd helped the young unknown to market and publish his stories.

In exile from the domain of his own fiction, Usman now turned from writing stories of social realism to retelling traditional tales from Punjab and Sind with a bitter tinge of political allusion. In the best of these (which set a standard for other writers), a farmer gave his daughter as a bride to a crocodile. She invited her family, one by one, to the crocodile kingdom in the depths of the river. They succumbed to its wealth and riches and decided to stay on. Finally only one was left on land, a youngest son. He went to visit his sister and her crocodile in-laws in the country beneath the water where he found his parents and siblings in residence. They had eaten crocodile bread, and they, too, were gradually metamorphosing into crocodiles.

His former editors couldn't understand the change in his style, but when he published 'The Prince of Crocodile Country' in the country's most popular children's magazine his young readers loved it. He continued to dip his bucket into the same well of folklore, though few of his later stories were ever as harsh, and some indulged themselves in a tear or two.

As he grew older, he found that the only effective means

to alleviate his sense of existential guilt was to help the deprived, in modest and even surreptitious ways. Rokeya, generous by nature, was aware of her husband's acts of kindness, and she, too, became adept at saving to give away whatever she could.

In the evenings, Usman would come home to find his wife, shalwar-kameez crushed and dopatta abandoned on some chair or peg, busy with a dozen chores – Shamyl on her hip, Saadi holding a finger, Rabia, the oldest, named after the saint of Basra whose story she had read and reread on the ship to Karachi, holding on to her hem and attempting to help. By that time Mai Rasulan, the woman who worked in the house all day as cook and nanny, would have gone home and Rokeya would be putting the finishing touches to the dinners she'd serve herself, of lentils, bread and two vegetables, small portions of chicken or mutton, with slivered carrots and chopped tomatoes in small dishes on the side (both she and Usman disliked raw onions). Rokeya would also have made sweets with her own hands, or prepared the salads Usman loved: chickpeas with tomatoes and tamarind, and segments of guava, banana, orange steeped in a wash of lemon juice, which she'd sprinkle with sugar, salt and black pepper, or decorate with sprigs of fresh mint.

7

During the day Rokeya worked in a primary school, where she had originally taught art before being promoted to teaching English grammar and composition as well. Though the British Council had tried to place her in one of the more expensive and well-paying schools that were popular with the children of diplomats, she had preferred to teach in a more modest local school only a few minutes' walk away from their lane. She had encountered some slight hostility at first, but in the end a mixed group of like-minded women, one among them the Italian wife of a Pakistani and another the daughter of a Pakistani father and an English mother, had succeeded in establishing their credentials as teachers in their liberal but righteous neighbourhood, and overcoming prejudice. And the fact that the English taught there was likely to be of a high standard encouraged neighbours to send their children to them for their primary schooling. Karachites, cultural nationalists though they might be, were realists to the bone as well; they thought that if their children were to have a Western education, they should also be well versed in the medium of its instruction.

Very occasionally, when Usman went to a talk at the Press

Club or some other official and male-dominated function at which they both knew she'd feel out of place, she'd go with friends to see a rehearsed reading by amateurs at the offices of the British Council, or a theatrical production by a visiting company of professional Shakespeareans from provincial English theatres. On such evenings, dressed in Western clothes her neighbour Tabinda would run up from patterns cut out of imported women's magazines, with her hair, now long, pulled back and knotted at the nape of her neck, she'd be introduced to the expatriate English community as Mrs Usman Ali, the wife of a respected local man of letters who'd once worked on the foreign desk of the *Telegraph*.

Her own pictures, too, had found a showroom. She had begun modestly, while the children slept, drawing figures of locals in wax crayon on old pieces of fabric. Tabinda ran a small dressmaking business from her house, which was expanding into one of the most successful concerns in the neighbourhood. She saw Rokeya's work and immediately said she'd take some pictures on a sale or return arrangement to display at her boutique, at which a number of handicrafts were sold.

In Tabinda, Rokeya had found the companion who made her feel entirely at home in the world she had chosen to inhabit. She was fascinated with her friend's expert needlework: she learned words like zardoz, karchob, salma sitara for the gold embroidery and sequin work with which Tabinda, spectacles slipping down her nose, could keep her fingers occupied as she talked. Tabinda also taught her to use herbal remedies to wash her hair, and powders and pastes of sandalwood and gram flour to cleanse her skin; to fry savoury fritters and make the halwas of carrot and pumpkin Usman and the little ones found so delicious. In exchange, Rokeya would teach her friend to bake cakes rich with cocoa, cheese twists, shortbread and lemon curd tarts, following recipes cut out from English magazines; Tabinda loved these. They gossiped in a mixture of languages – Rokeya using an English word when she couldn't find the right one in Urdu, Tabinda, who understood English well but wouldn't speak it, supplying her with its translation.

With Tabinda, Rokeya also shopped for the bric-à-brac she used to decorate her house. Blue and white tiles from Thatta, pots of brass and earthenware and ceramic jars, hangings of interwoven colours, dull and bright, that she draped over a bed or a chest or the back of a chair, camel skin lampshades, low stools of wood and rope or of the softest leather, little rugs she used in place of carpets.

Another neighbour was chic, short-haired, chain-smoking Jahan Bano Kazmi, known to her friends as Jani, a rich young widow who, to console herself in her bereavement, had established *Endeavour*, a glossy but progressive English-language magazine, with her own funds. She ran it, as Managing Editor, from the glass-enclosed portico of her sprawling villa on top of the hill, which also housed the neighbourhood's finest collections of novels, biographies and histories in English. Rokeya and Jani lived on parallel lanes but, in that odd Karachi way, Rokeya's next-door neighbours were petty government officials while Jani's house was flanked by the palatial residence of an ex-President's family and the smaller but very smart house of a German diplomat. You couldn't imagine two women more different from each other than shy, traditional Tabinda and convent-educated, English-speaking Jani. Yet they were friends.

Jani saw Rokeya's thick chalky drawings of children against dark backgrounds on display at Tabinda's boutique. She wondered who the naive artist was who'd done them. Tabinda explained that they'd been drawn by Rokeya, the respected intellectual Usman Ali's English wife. Jani immediately asked to meet Rokeya, commissioned her at first to illustrate stories, articles and features for *Endeavour*, and then to write reviews of art exhibitions and related events under a pseudonym which Rokeya never divulged to Usman.

Rokeya had noticed that magazine illustrations here tended to copy the example of Western comic-strips and commercial art. Children, particularly, appeared like little Western youngsters with dark wigs on. Working with inks, coloured pencils and crayons to avoid the mess and waste of paint, using strokes or blocks of colour to contrast with black-and-white and empty spaces, she developed a vernacular idiom of her own, inspired in equal parts by the modern figurative painting she saw at the exhibitions Usman took her to, and the lively, beautiful countenances of the children she observed around her. An early effort,

'Children and Gulmohar Trees', a composition in vibrant green, reds and oranges with a clever use of white spaces, which depicted four local children playing ball in a garden by an artificial pond, became particularly popular as a motif on napkins, tablecloths and wall hangings.

At first she went around with a sketch-pad, following the rules of her training which decreed that every picture should be copied from life. But then she realised that her earnest demeanour alienated her models and caused her to be seen as an eccentric or a curiosity – the observer observed. Photographs? Far worse, Usman warned her: the children of the street might be amused, and chase after her without malice, but many adults would feel their privacy invaded. She learnt how right he was when she tried to snap a beggar dressed in white flowing robes with several strings of brightly coloured beads around his neck and long, oiled locks sitting on his shoulders like little snakes; she was cursed and pursued by the stick-brandishing mendicant. She took to recording details in words instead, or using the camera of her mind.

At home, she'd draw furiously from her notes, scribbled or memorised. Her own three children would serve as models, as they had done in that best-known work of hers. They were a constant source of inspiration; as she chronicled them growing, her colours and forms acquired movement and a disarming, almost garish vitality. Usman wouldn't sit for her as himself, but when she asked him to stand in for a fruit vendor or watchman she wanted to fit into a local scene, he'd sportingly crouch or kneel until she had captured a required pose.

Abstract expressionism, geometric forms and compositions that exalted colour were hugely fashionable here, but Rokeya had little time for a trend that reminded her of dated Western modes she wanted to leave behind. She preferred the local handicrafts, embroidery and ceramics of various kinds, and found the gap between the traditional artisan and the modern artist dismaying. For a time, she also tried to emulate the former, painting pictures of fishing boats in their harbours and buffaloes in their ponds in gilt outlines against a black backdrop, in imitation of the style of a popular Bengali folk artist, thinking they might sell quite well. She soon discarded them as unsatisfactory. Her interest was in capturing, with a few swift strokes and echoes of colour, the relationship between figures and the landscapes they inhabited.

Jani liked Rokeya's pictures, the low prices she charged and her self-deprecating attitude to her work. Locals, when they discovered Rokeya Usman Ali was originally a Londoner, found it hard to believe that a foreigner could survey the local scene with so intimate and affectionate an eye. But from time to time Jani would say, 'Lydia dear' (she was one of the few friends who refused to call her Rokeya) 'Lydia dear, must you make your little ones quite so dark?'

Rokeya offered her illustrations to Usman for his magazine, but in spite of her efforts to create an idiom that was fresh and local, he gently ignored her submissions, preferring to employ a male artist whose sketches Rokeya thought were drab and pretentious.

8

A drink-sodden writer who was producing a serial in several parts for *Endeavour* had failed to deliver the current month's instalment. Rokeya, who had already done the illustration for it, decided, when Jani asked her to translate one of Usman's stories to fill the empty pages, to write a story of her own. 'A Day at the Seaside' was inspired by that illustration: a couple in remote outline walking by a single sapphire stroke of sea, with a semicircle of red sun floating above.

Rokeya's story was about a young woman who, bored and lonely during one of her husband's many absences, agreed to spend some hours at the beach with one of his friends. Bedazzled by sun and sand, she let him kiss her, but then, at sunset, she asked to be taken home. What happened in the hours between was left to the reader's imagination.

She was pleased with it; she thought she'd learnt Usman's lesson well. Her prose was simple to the point of bareness. Descriptions were brief and tactile: hot sand, salty sea, cloud-streaked sky, a sultry May day on Karachi's beach.

Jani read the story in just twenty minutes, sitting on her tiled patio by the lily pond which party guests, mistaking it for a carpet, often walked into. Rokeya watched her expression, sipping iced coffee through a plastic straw from a tall, frosted glass. When she was done, Jani frowned, lit a gold-tipped mentholated cigarette, then handed one to Rokeya. 'Mmm. Certainly not Usman's, this. A bit ... mmm ... like imitation Somerset Maugham. It has some promise, but it shouldn't end so abruptly, and why don't the characters have names?'

When Rokeya suggested she'd call the woman Parveen and the man Captain Mansur, Jani remarked with one eyebrow raised: 'Oh, I assumed they were both foreigners. English, actually.'

That night, as they sat on the veranda sipping cardamom-scented green tea after dinner, Rokeya showed Usman the story and relayed Jani's comments to him, presenting it as the work of a novice without telling him who'd written it.

'Mediocre.' He frowned. 'Very amateurish. Even for a woman's magazine. Second-grade Somerset Maugham, your Jani is right. Why these writers don't give their characters names is beyond me, when they name beaches with such parochial precision. But I like your picture of the figures by the sea.'

Rokeya felt that he'd guessed who the writer was. The story remained unpublished.

She also asked Usman, after Jani suggested it to her, that they work together on a translation of some of his fables for *Endeavour*. A story she particularly liked was about two neighbours. One was the master of seven vineyards, the other only owned a date palm. Yet the rich man resented the fruit of his neighbour's tree. Since Usman hadn't written anything original for a while, she thought the labour of changing his story from one language to another might revive his interest in his work, which had suffered from his readers' neglect and then from his resulting indifference. (He trusted his English even less than in his London days; her spoken Urdu, though fluent, was ungrammatical, and she hadn't ever learned to read the language very well.)

To her surprise, he agreed.

They spent many hours together over several evenings, returning to the rapt companionship of their early years, arguing about choices of words, paragraphs, tenses. Instead of translating his words literally, she'd ask him to retell them to her, unadorned. Rokeya began to weave Usman's words, as he said them, into a single tapestry of many parables and images even richer and stranger than the tales he'd originally told. She'd ask for the names of his unnamed characters, or give the protagonists of the stories their own names and the names of people they knew. And then, one evening, the final draft of their work was done, so well that it satisfied even Usman's severe standard.

9

Rokeya was in a quandary. She enjoyed her teaching, but Jani had offered her something better. Now a member of parliament, Jani travelled regularly to her constituency and also to Rawalpindi for meetings of the National Assembly. She no longer had time to run the magazine with the dedication and energy it needed, and wanted Rokeya to take over, as her deputy, the day-to-day management of editorial issues. She was offering a salary of 350 rupees a month, more than Rokeya earned at the school, and the working day would be shorter, too, as many of her jobs could be done at home. Rokeya could continue to teach art twice a week, at the school or privately.

Jani had another reason to spend time away from Karachi. Her unhappily married lover, whose secret second wife she was planning to become, was also a member of parliament, and she could spend time with him discreetly on her trips away – here in this city, the presence of a stranger in her life would be noticed and speculated upon, but away from home, 'in the eye of the storm' as she put it, people were less likely to care.

The end of the collaboration with Usman had left Rokeya

wanting something more and different, as if there was a canvas waiting to be filled with form and colour. What would his response be when he learnt about Jani's offer? Would he shrug and say, Do whatever you like, dear? Or would he encourage her to make the change? He'd never, ever let her feel that she needed to bring home any money; it was understood that she should do whatever she pleased with what she earned, and if she chose to spend it on the children – well, that was her privilege. On the other hand, he didn't approve of her constant shifts of interest and focus, evidently didn't think she was good with words, and would have preferred her to concentrate on her painting.

Today had been one of those grey and cloudy Karachi days that offered some reprieve: an absent sun, a slight breeze and even a hint of rain in the air. In the late afternoon, as usual, she had taken her sketch-pad out to the veranda which she used in all seasons as her studio, as the children frolicked in the garden, spraying each other with water from a green rubber pipe. Now early evening shadows were deepening on the freshly cut grass. But her usual ideas were playing her false: the children, the flowers, a deep blue kite wheeling very close to a cloud.

She had been thinking, for some time, of England: was it, perhaps, time for a visit? Did she owe it to Rabia, Saadi and Shamyl to show them the places their mother had known as a child?

How would things be in London now? Would she feel at home there? Her father sent her courteous missives on special occasions; Jack wrote from time to time, but even he couldn't convey what she wanted to know.

Did she really miss anything in England, besides the late spring weather? After all, she had so much here to replace what she had left behind. And if she had stayed on, would she ever have remained in London, and wouldn't her life in some country village have been far quieter than what she had found here? And had she even changed, or only settled?

She had thought that she'd need to use Urdu here most of the time but, in fact, most of her friends and acquaintances were English speaking, and she spoke her mother tongue more often than the language she'd taken pains to learn. At first, she'd had occasion to practise her newly acquired language with Tabinda, her closest friend. Over the years, though, it was the company of Jani she had come to rely on – Jani, who, with her Westernised tastes and perfect English, was as much at home in London, where she spent alternate summers with her brother, as in Karachi. For the rest Rokeya's social life, though sporadic, centred largely around the activities of the expatriate community and the British Council.

As a critic she also retained a lively interest in local art and artists, and somewhere, secretly, aspired to be counted among them. When she'd first arrived here, two of the best-known women painters, Anna Molka and Esther Rahim, were the European wives of Pakistani men, attempting to adjust their painterly vision to their new country. Some years ago, when an American action painter had dropped her bright wares like a time-bomb on the local scene, several local artists had decided that spontaneous outbursts of colourful abstraction were the richest expression of the nation's new energy and aspirations. (Later, a rumour had spread that the visiting lady was a secret agent, sent to Pakistan to rally young artists to Uncle Sam's cause.) Younger women artists, trained abroad, had returned to paint in Karachi: Zubeida Agha, who was Rokeya's exact contemporary, but for her sensuous taste the undoubtedly gifted artist's vision was too rarefied; Laila Javeri, with her bold canvases; and Naz Ikramullah, Jani's favourite, who had exhibited her work at the age of twenty-one to excitement and acclaim. So much to write about – but, as a painter, would she, could she ever fit?

Weeks ago, Rokeya had planned a series of new gouaches called 'Houses', a view of the neighbourhood seen from the top of the hill where their house was: a composition of contrasts between the geometry of architectural forms and the vague riot of floral colours. Tentatively, she had returned to her paintbox. But the years of working with pencils, to fulfil a commission to deadline, had diminished her confidence in her use of paints, the medium she had always wanted to make her own.

Today, she had put a raw green mango on a plate, which she'd placed on a low table, and thought she'd sketch a still life to illustrate an article about mango puddings and drinks Jani had dashed off that morning. I am coming to the end of something, she thought as she sketched. Somehow, over the ten years of her life in Karachi, she'd become too busy with the demands of her own full day, the need to practise economies, the children's demands and wants, the hectic serenity she'd found. Her social life and Usman's had begun to diverge to the extent that there was hardly any occasion they attended as a couple. There were the rare but regular dinners with Jani, at which her husband discussed politics and books with their hostess, and the evenings they spent with Tabinda and her husband Umar, when after an early and delicious dinner the men wandered off to read and comment on each other's manuscripts while the women sipped green tea in sleepy companionship.

The only time Rokeya spent alone with Usman was in the last hours of the evening, when he would listen silently or with the odd comment or question as she narrated the events of her day. But recently – yesterday evening – he had responded to what she thought was an amusing anecdote about a fruit vendor who'd come to the kitchen door and tried to sell her a single mango for a rupee with an impatient, 'Can't you let me have my tea in peace before you jump on me with your complaints about the thieving natives?' The point of her story was going to be that she'd bought the mango only because she was so intrigued by its shape she wanted to paint it.

What had happened to their unending conversation? For many years she'd consulted him about her decisions, occupied herself with his comforts, supplemented his earnings with her own, enjoyed his presence beside her in bed awake or asleep, depended on his involvement in every aspect of her life, felt rejected when he came home and, burying himself in some tome of Ghalib, Tolstoy or Dostoevsky, seemed to ignore her need for company, or responded to her easy flow of anecdotes about children and work with an abruptness that sometimes bordered on cruelty. But somehow – she knew this now – she had ceased to ask him about himself, lost the questions she might put to him about his fears or his needs, as if by doing so she would be an intruder in some very private place, a hermitage with a firmly barred door.

And in some moment she could no longer retrieve, she'd ceased to see the man who had given her his empty and inhabited spaces to transform into her own, been her harbour, her oasis, her magic carpet to a longed-for land. She'd talked on and on to fill the silence that swelled between them because she felt that by regaling him with the trivia of her day she was keeping him close to her, taking his usual complacency for contentment. But she'd lost the gift of those words that had bound him to her over distances of latitude and longitude.

She remembered how, one day, she'd been sketching in the garden and, suddenly thirsty, had gone to fetch a full glass of cooled water she thought she'd left on the veranda. She'd found it half empty and thought that one of the children must have sipped from it. But when she sipped from it, the water tasted slightly brackish. Had someone changed the glass? Or was it yesterday she'd left it there, and somehow missed a day?

She finished her sketch, and stood back. Not bad at all.

But something was still missing. She knew what she should do. She'd leave the table and the plate as they were, a network of grey-black charcoal lines, but she'd fill in the colours of the mango: instead of painting it green, as it appeared to the eye in real life, she'd give it the rich gold tones it would have acquired if it had been left to ripen on its branch. And next to it she'd place some fallen flower petals.

She went in to fetch her new paintbox.

10

Even if she'd thought of asking him, Usman would not have found the words to tell Rokeya this: what he missed most was the way she'd spontaneously drawn a bird catcher's net of tales around him, which, in turn, had served to enmesh his own stories with wings still flapping. Now, when he came home and saw her immersed in practicalities, or when she recounted her day's preoccupations and chores, he envied the cheerful pleasure she took in everything, even in complaining; envied the affection her friends and the care her children and even their pets demanded from her; envied the attention she paid to her pictures. (He'd only once seen her cry, and that was when her father's annual birthday card arrived on the 1st of May, three weeks late for her birthday.)

Now, it seemed to him, he was just another colourful motif in the mural of her tranquillity, not its maker as he once would unquestioningly have thought he was. There was something he resented in this contentment. Everything so casual, so enthusiastic, so full of excess energy. Lydia, he reflected, seemed to have left him; he wasn't sure how well he knew this bustling, practical Rokeya who had taken her place.

He was fifty-three. Though his grey hair had receded

slightly, it was still abundant; but his belly, flanks and thighs were heavier, his ankles weak, his quick step slower. His twin sons by his first wife were estranged from him. His own literary career was still going slowly. In a climate where, after nationalism's first surge had subsided and literature could be considered a vocation or a pastime rather than the presentation of a manifesto, he was frequently compared by Westernised critics to Flaubert and to Zola; other, younger writers emulated Kafka, Camus and Robbe-Grillet. Denying Western influence, insisting that he drew on local rather than imported traditions, he was placed in a category of his own as a regionalist or a man of letters who wrote for a select audience composed almost exclusively of other writers.

As a young man, he had briefly hoped that Gorki and Sholokhov would take the place of his beloved Tolstoy and Dostoevsky. But in recent years the Soviet fictions that were available here in translation had moved on from the farm and the tractor to the hearthside contentment of married couples after a day of work in the factory, to the awakening social conscience of youth in the post-Stalin years they referred to as the Thaw. He wished he could find the will to write narratives of that bland and reassuring simplicity. But he found no inspiration in these saccharine stories with their puppet characters, designed to sweeten the prescribed doses of material and industrial progress: their transparency was false.

In Usman's first novel, published before Partition, he had told the story of a youth who travels from rural Punjab to Delhi and Lahore; he falls in love with a rich and lovely Bengali Kayastha girl who is active in the Freedom Movement and eventually breaks his heart. Rediscovered some years ago by a new generation hungry for adventure and romance, it was now available everywhere in a bright-covered new edition, the fourth in as many years, and continued to sell in impressive numbers to housewives and the young.

A work he dismissed as immature and sentimental, its language made him feel as if he'd spilt pomegranate juice over the novel's pages and they were still sticky with it. He had never even been in love when he wrote it. That came later. When he moved to Karachi, he had met Ameena Durrani at a writers' gathering. A recent refugee from central India, she was shy and almost clumsy in her movements. But her soft speech and gentle appearance grew on him. She was also a feminist and an almost shockingly powerful writer, whose work, he would have thought, had been written by an experienced older man, not a young woman so recently out of purdah. They would meet occasionally at writers' gatherings; more often, they exchanged long letters about the stories she sent him to read. Their exchanges soon stretched to include the state of literature, of the world. Once, he thought he recognised something he had said about himself in one of her stories; once in a note she expressed something that might be taken for interest in him, or even affection. He had responded in a tone that was avuncular and also faintly dismissive. He was sixteen years older, and married:

even if he had overcome his scruples and proposed to her, he assumed from her writings that she'd never become a second wife, as her older sister, a painter, had, to her chagrin. Some time before he left for London he had heard that she'd become a rich landlord's second wife. He hadn't heard from her or seen her again. She lived in Lahore; though hardly prolific, she was a respected writer, and had won a prize for her first novel.

He would never write a story about her. But had he experienced the tenderness he felt for her before he wrote his first novel, that sentimental work might have had more depth. He had considered rewriting it, and even carried a copy to London with that task in mind, but boredom soon set in. He hadn't particularly wanted to see it back in print in its unrevised state. But Chowdhry Sahib had insisted that this new edition of an old hit might attract a new generation of readers to his more recent work. His two volumes of mature short stories had not, however, sold more than two or three hundred copies each, his new novel was incomplete, his job at the magazine not taxing but often tedious.

Once he had asked Rokeya: 'Can't you stop dabbling and concentrate on one thing? Your gouaches? Do you really want to keep on wasting your talent on illustrations for women's magazines? Can't you gather enough of your paintings for a show? Surely the British Council will do it if those snobs at the Arts Council won't have you? What do you really want to do?'

She looked puzzled.

'Do? Nothing, really, but it's all so much fun.'

For her, and for their children, he felt an aching tenderness that filled him when he was away from them for even a few hours. When he was with them, though, he was at best inexpressive and at worst irascible. (After acquiring a pair of budgerigars and then a pregnant rabbit that gave birth as soon as they had brought her home, the children had become attached to a hen Mai Rasulan bought for the pot; they insisted on letting it into the house to sleep on their beds. There were times when the budgies' incessant cheeping, the hen's intrusion into his space, or the sight of rabbits' droppings all over the veranda, would make him scold even Rabia, his favourite.)

Rokeya seemed even keener than he that Rabia, Saadi and Shamyl should have a secure grounding in Urdu and a strong sense of cultural identity, and prevailed on him to help them to master the national language. Often, he'd come home to find her regaling them with children's tales he'd written, but she read by rote or retold from memory, and she constantly remoulded the grammar and syntax into her own eccentric idiom. The tales, too, would be reinvented: a frog would become an enchanted princess, a village boy would be transformed into an intrepid traveller or a little girl in a garden turn into a brave heroine, and the unnamed figures of folklore would acquire the names of the members of their own little family. But the children are always asking what the characters are called! she'd say when he accused her of freely intermingling fact with fantasy. He would take over from her, reading or telling the stories himself, and then asking the children to read out passages aloud, or to take dictation.

But he knew that in contrast to her garrulous approach he made it all seem too much like homework, and often found himself impatient with the two boys, the older of whom, Saadi, at nearly seven, had particular difficulties with the Urdu script, and held his brother Shamyl back too. (Nine-year-old Rabia, on the other hand, had mastered Urdu and was learning to read the Qur'an at Tabinda's knee.) Saadi would constantly refer to masculine objects as feminine and vice versa; a book and a chair would become masculine, water and yoghurt feminine. He would misspell Arabic words that used letters such as 'ain' and 'suad' and, like his mother, he would ask why they needed to be there at all since they had lost their original sound values. Usman soon stopped supervising their lessons, wondering, not without anxiety, whether one, or both, of his sons would want one day to explore their English roots, and leave the country of their birth for their mother's native land.

One day Shamyl had come home in a state of distress: a group of older boys had called his brother a Current, which was a derogatory word for a local Christian, because of Saadi's hesitant Urdu and the pale, freckled skin and reddish hair he had inherited from his Scottish grandmother. 'If

Saadi's a Current, I must be one too,' he wept. Usman was unable to console him. But he took a guilty pleasure in the reflection of himself he saw in Shamyl's coppery skin and abundant black hair.

It was a handicap, Usman reminded Rokeya, that their children had a mother who spoke her children's native language with little respect for grammar or syntax, mangling verbs and cases and always unable to grasp the intricacies of gender.

'Well,' she retorted, 'at least I chatter away, and read signs and headlines; more than you can say for Jani. Or Rasulan, who can't utter a phrase without a mistake. And it wasn't I who chose to send them to an English-medium school.'

All of this was true. Like many other bourgeois Karachi ladies of their acquaintance, Jani was as honest about her lack of fluency in Urdu as she was comfortable in her English idiom, and, though she read the national language reasonably well, would hardly choose to speak it at all; Rasulan's language was Sindhi, in which she had sung lullabies to the children since each of them was born. And Usman himself had sent Saadi and Shamyl to the English-medium Lady Jennings School at the other end of town where the standard of Urdu taught was given no importance; from there, when they were slightly older, they would transfer to the prestigious and expensive Grammar School. Rabia still studied at the local PECHS girls' school, a short walk away from their house. Neither parent was keen for the children to attend St Patrick's, the Roman Catholic school for boys, though sending them there would have cost them less.

At night, he was again plagued by those odd dreams that had made him shake himself awake in his youth: he was climbing a ladder to the sky which ended in an empty space without a bridge to the platform he was trying to reach, and was left dangling in mid-air; he had entered a formal occasion shirtless, or with no shoes on; he was crouching on a street, desperate to relieve himself or trying to conceal the fact that he was wearing no trousers.

He took to sleeping on a pallet on the veranda; on certain nights he'd take it into the garden and wander into a fragile sleep, breathing in the air heavy with the scent of flowers that only bloomed in darkness.

He had ceased to torment himself as much as he would once have done about the political situation. On more than one occasion had found himself in grudging agreement with some supporter of General Ayub Khan's military-backed regime who said that things were improving and would continue to improve, there were signs of prosperity and progress, and wasn't a little reticence or discretion a small price to pay? He sidestepped an argument with radical young Umar about the current political situation on more than one occasion. But in the work of writing, which continued to rise like a glass barrier between him and everything he loved, he was still aware of his old and overriding search for perfection;

every phrase was an almost impossible challenge, and writing an entire story the most onerous of responsibilities.

He was, in middle age, beset with the old feeling of being left behind in every part of life, and in his career most of all. He had recently written a long story about a Western anthropologist who, while she befriended villagers on the pretext of collecting and transcribing the unwritten tales they passed down from generation to generation, sent her colleagues to desecrate their ancient cemetery in search of antique tiles, ancient potsherds and human bones. He knew it was one of the very best creations of his mature years. Contenders were being selected for a prestigious literary prize, and he knew that Jani, who had the ear of one of the judges, would be speaking for him, but how could he ever hope to win? Even in the rank of regional writers to which, for all his years in big cities, he was invariably delegated, he stood far behind Shah Bilal in acclaim and appeal. His stories for children had been his most successful work for many years; here, too, Bilal had outdone him with a volume of nationalist lyrics for young readers and a collection of tales (mostly lifted from retellings by Flora Annie Steel) that he claimed his old village grandmother had told him by a winter fire.

His relationships were shadowed. Chowdhry, avuncular as he was, took him for granted. Umar had his own left-wing interests, and Jani was above all his wife's friend. Rokeya, until she became a mother, had placed him above all else; now he came second to their children, for whom she showed an almost feral devotion, reading to them, playing with them, teaching them to draw, working only while they were at school to spend every available hour with them. And though he recognised his children's affection for him from the way they clung to his knees when he came home and the tranquillity in their eyes when he kissed them in their beds or held their little fingers as he prayed over them when they fell ill, he couldn't pretend for an instant that he could lay claim to an atom of the need they had for her.

Yes, he stood in second (if not third) place, in every walk of life. Except when someone depended on him, or something was wanted from him. Advice, editorial or professional, to a fledgling writer. A word in the right ear, to get a young journalist a job. Even the redoubtable Chowdhry Sahib, to whom he owed so much, who called him 'son' and depended on him more than on his own children, had laden him with administrative responsibilities at the magazine that were increasing by the month – commissioning, chasing and editing copy and, worse still, juggling and stretching financial resources. His job cramped his imagination, punctured his urge to write.

Companionship and inspiration, not dependency and duty, were what he had wanted. Again and again, he had to remind himself of the words of the Sura Rahman, to which, as he grew older, he often turned for succour: 'How many of your Lord's favours will you deny?' I am grateful, I truly am, for all that God has given us, he would tell himself. Then what is it I miss?

He had read again and again the verses in the Book that said the sky was our canopy and the earth our bed; the rain came down to water grain and grape, the seed and the sapling were all signs of the Maker's grace. Why then couldn't he see the beauty of the bird on the wing, no longer hear its song of praise? Why, when, had the old yearnings that had driven him turned from desire into discontent?

Then there were the refrains of nationally acclaimed poets like Bilal, who sang on about the New Dawn and the Blessed Golden Soil of the Promised Land, and made him impatient and cynical. Usman loved his country right or wrong and would never ever leave it, but its soil was still pitted with the graves of martyrs and victims. The new dawn, he thought, had yet to deliver most of its promises of the glorious day to come.

Only once, he had had his doubts and hesitations voiced to him by someone else, before he had become entirely aware of them. That was when Jani had responded to a chance remark of his about providence: 'Luck? You believe in it? Consider yourself fortunate? I think the only thing you've ever had on your side is your own fortitude. And yes, you were lucky to meet Lydia, too.' He'd been startled then, because he'd always seen the chain of events that had led him to where he was as luck, but now he could see that good fortune and fate were not necessarily identical.

In imperceptible stages he had let himself become the

doleful, guarded man he had been so many years before. But there was a difference. He was more silent, more guarded, than he'd ever been in that London he and Lydia had made their own, light years ago when he'd met her and learnt to love her. Even when he spoke to himself, it was of distant matters.

He decided that the story Rokeya had translated into English as simple and lucid as his own Urdu was too good for *Endeavour*. Without telling her, he submitted it for publication in a government-sponsored anthology edited by a leading, and arrogant, littérateur who told him how good he thought it was, and asked for more such translations, saying that the publishers would be proud to produce a collection of his fiction for foreign readers.

Rokeya's expressive face immediately revealed how disappointed she was in him for making the choice without consulting her. He tried to lessen her dismay by telling her that she'd get sole credit for the translation; most of the work, after all, had been hers. But when, after a period of silence, she suggested that they work together on others to make up a volume, or offered to turn his folktales into a book in English, he responded with words that she took as his tactful dismissal.

11

One night, he had refused to go with her to a performance of *Henry V*, for which she'd acquired two tickets. 'Spare me your English kings, Plantagenets or Tudors,' he'd muttered, a little spitefully. She went without him, asking anglophile Jani to take his place.

She'd come back at midnight. He was alone; the children, when he went to pick them up from Tabinda's house, had fallen asleep in her daughter's room, and she insisted he shouldn't wake them. He was still up, correcting galleys, and looked through the open window when he heard the growl of a car in the lane to see her alight from an unfamiliar grey Volkswagen instead of Jani's dark blue Opel Kapitan.

'Richard,' she responded when he asked her who'd brought her home. 'Jani had a headache; she left at the intermission.'

'And where was Claire?'

Uncharacteristically, he'd remembered the name of one of her English friends.

'She's gone home to Suffolk for two months,' she said. 'This season never suits her.'

❧

A few weeks later, he talked to her in the evening, for the first time since they'd collaborated on the translation, about a story he was writing.

'It's about a woman who, bored and lonely during one of her husband's absences, agrees to spend a day at the seaside with a male acquaintance. They become lovers for the day. As the story ends, the woman, ashamed, is wondering whether to tell her husband about the mistake she's made. The woman is Austrian, the wife of a much older diplomat and herself a painter, her lover's a weedy Englishman in a white suit, with gin and tobacco on his breath. I'm not going to specify the husband's nationality. The setting is Alexandria, the time the present.'

'Wherever did you get such an idea from? People we know? Has Jani been gossiping? Not ... Richard and Claire, surely?'

Usman wondered whether she was being disingenuous or deliberately obtuse in refusing to bite the bait he'd cast.

'You tell me,' he snapped.

She blanched. 'You didn't think that Richard and I ... Oh, Mr Usman, of all the ideas!'

Then, uncontrollably, he was laughing at her outraged innocence.

'My dearest, it's only my elaboration of that story you wrote some months ago. I found it in my drawer the other day and thought it had potential. So I stole your plot.'

At dawn he was up before anyone else, just as he'd often

risen before Rokeya in the early days of his marriage when he'd wanted to write before he left for work. Strolling on the veranda with a cigarette between his fingers and looking at the brightening sky, he found himself remembering how, all those years ago, they'd spent their wedding night together, neither of them inexperienced yet both guileless and, in some odd way, untouched and virginal – and how then, and for years after, that bare discovery of each other, the erasure between their bodies of all but the final barriers of bone, had seen them through, made poverty appear to be austerity, need anticipation, disappointment mere lack of opportunity.

In her ineffable manner (he thought) she has always been wise: in refusing to see what is intended to strew bitterness in her field of vision, in avoiding paths where others spread frustration. While he'd worried over writer's block and unwritten masterpieces, unattained goals and rewards ungained, money never earned and fame's elusiveness, she had in some odd way retained the innocence and wonder of the childhood she'd never had, and even when he'd withheld his love from her, this woman who had orphaned and dispossessed herself for him continued to trust in him as if he were a beloved, negligent parent. The carefree, sometimes insensitive manner in which she continued to conduct her day, her pretence that he was the sole provider while she regularly and significantly supplemented his income, her seeming unconcern for that chronic exhaustion of his which bordered on despair – all this was her gift to him, the gift of valuing what she could have dismissed as the transience of their shared existence, the gift of faith she had in the life they had made for each other.

He had thought, for a time, that love could too easily fall prey to duty and responsibility, flinch under its own burden, lose its origin in the weightless places of the heart. But he knew now that without the burden of responsibility love couldn't survive: love was its own weight, its own task.

Barefoot, he stepped onto the wet grass, dew washing his feet. He made towards the gulmohar tree, which dominated the narrow garden; it wouldn't be in flower for a while, though tight new buds were appearing on its branches. A few days ago he had desultorily leafed through Rokeya's sketch book which she'd left on the veranda, open and fluttering in the morning breeze. He'd wondered, then, whether her bright impressions of the tree, her children and their garden were plans for more ambitious works which, like so much of what she planned, would remain unfinished, fading away on the canvas of her mind. Now, as if one of her sketches had come to life, a half-submerged memory of some evening he'd come home before sunset unfolded like a storyteller's painted scroll before him in the empty garden: Saadi sitting cross-legged on the rug beneath the tree, managing to read, with a measure of success, an entire page of his Urdu primer; Shamyl standing over his shoulder and prompting him; Rabia perched on a branch above eating the tender petals of its blossom, which she said tasted like tamarind; Rokeya on the veranda, wiping her forehead with a paint-smeared hand as she swiftly filled her blank canvas with leafless branches laden with scarlet flowers like little flames, calling out to him when she heard the door shut behind him and his footsteps in the hall: 'Are you home, Mr Usman?'

'The vision of a flower teaches the eye to rejoice in every colour.' For years Usman had struggled with this concept of Ghalib's. He had even started and then abandoned work on an essay about the mystic ghazal by the great poet which culminated in that verse. But eyes, Usman had commented, were the greatest deceivers; they showed you colours you couldn't aspire to, dreams that filled you with boundless longing. Longing led to loss, loss to lamentation and mourning. The very poem by Ghalib he was discussing was full of clouds and rain and tears of separation; pain, it said, must break its boundaries to become its own palliative.

Was it necessary, then, to weep before you recognised joy? Year after year, the tight little buds of the gulmohar tree had unfurled into gold and scarlet flames on their branches while he barely noticed, their colours just beyond their reach because the field of his vision was too restricted to contain them. Had he, who had never wept after his mother died, who had left no trace of a footstep on the road away from his past, had he remained blind to all the colours around him and, if so, for how long? But then he remembered how the night before he left London a tear or two had trickled down his cheek, and how she, the woman he had learned to love without knowing how to tell her, had taken his tears as the token she'd been waiting for, the sign that he didn't want to leave her.

He didn't write the story about the lovers by the sea; he'd never really intended to. Instead, he spent three days working on a long, tender story about his wife's friend Tabinda – how, just a few years ago, Tabinda's journalist husband Umar had been arrested for inciting dissidence in his writings and spent forty days in jail before brave Tabinda succeeded in bailing him out. It became the centrepiece of *Puzzled Angels*, the collection of seven stories, one for each day of the week, that he wrote in a little over seven months, often staying up all night over several cups of tea and entire packs of cigarettes. Most of the stories were sour-sweet vignettes of married life, and of the struggle of ordinary people to survive in the difficult times of Martial Law. His wife drew a picture or two for every story.

He dedicated the book to Rokeya, who had once been called Lydia.

That dedication to her is one of the pieces Rokeya Javashvili-Usman Ali and her son Saadi Ali will include in a volume of her husband's favourite stories they co-edit after his death in 1984.

In this fragment of memory only a few hundred words long, Usman relives the day he received one of his country's most prestigious awards for his contributions to children's literature, consisting of a medal and a great deal of cash.

'... Or we could take a holiday,' he says to his English wife, who is painting the finishing touches to an arrangement of green, red and yellow swirls which she says is her impression of their three children at play in their garden, spraying each other with a water hose.

'To the hills? When the children's holidays start? Murree? Or Swat, perhaps? You could write, the children could learn to ride ponies, I could draw children playing against the backdrop of trees and lakes and hills, maybe even take my paints and do a watercolour, figures in a landscape ...'

'I was thinking of Topkapi, the Pyramids, the Vatican, the Alhambra ... and we could go back to London, if you like ...'

Usman realises that his wife has been away from her homeland for ten years; with all the expenses of daily living, they've never been able to afford the fare back.

'But my dearest Mr Usman,' she says. 'What a dreamer you are! First we have to build an annexe to the house, which seems to be getting smaller every day. The children are growing and we need at least two more rooms. Then Mai Rasulan's daughter is getting married, surely we should be giving her something, after all the years she's cooked for us and cared for the children – we're the only family she has, after all. And by the way, that path between our garden and the neighbours' wall is being used as a lavatory – yes, a lavatory! – by their watchman's children. Rasulan's nephew Shabbir who works for a contractor came to see me, and he says he can build a wall for us too and bring that strip of ground, that doesn't really belong to anyone, into our garden. I want a low brick wall we can whitewash, no barbed wire or bits of glass. We could plant another gulmohar tree to mark the boundary. You could write in its shade. Tell me, how on earth can we go wandering abroad when there's so much to be done right here? Actually, I was thinking ...'

'What were you thinking, dear?'

'Would you mind terribly if we just stayed home this summer? We could always wait and visit the hills next year ...'

Acknowledgements

Sections of *Another Gulmohar Tree* as a work in progress appeared in *Moving Worlds* and *The International Literary Quarterly*. I'd like to thank the editors, Shirley Chew and Peter Robertson respectively, for their interest.

Several friends read various drafts of this story. I'd especially like to thank Ruth and Sunetra for their support and interest from start to finish, Alev, for a perceptive reading of the first draft, Mary Flanagan for asking how the house was furnished, Ritu Menon for wanting to know more about women and painting, and Alison Fell for a close scrutiny of the near-final version. And in chronological order, the book's earliest readers, Mimi Khalvati, Peter Middleton, Githa Hariharan, Asif Farrukhi, Palash Mehrotra, Sujala Singh, Clare Colvin, Eibhlin Evans, Anita Mir, Anne-Marie Drosso and Bina Shah, for the responses and companionship a storyteller needs.

Thanks, too, to the team at Telegram: particularly Rebecca O'Connor for her subtle and inspiring readings, for gently eliciting and placing the prelude, and for giving me a writing year; and Lynn Gaspard for her rare combination of infectious enthusiasm and unstinting perfectionism in the days before publication. And last not but not least, Lara Frankena.

Aamer Hussein
London, November 2008